BLOOD LINE

KEVIN BROOKS

Barrington Stoke

First published in 2004 in Great Britain by
Barrington Stoke Ltd
18 Walker Street, Edinburgh, EH3 7LP

www.barringtonstoke.co.uk

This edition published 2015

Text © 2004 Kevin Brooks

A CIP catalogue record for this book is
available from the British Library upon
request

ISBN: 978-1-78112-491-8

Printed in China by Leo

CONTENTS

CHAPTER 1
NO SUMMER IN HERE

I don't know about you, but when I read a story I like to know what's going on right from the start. I don't need to know *everything*. I don't want to know about stuff that doesn't come into the story. But I need to know what's going on right from the first page. I want facts. I want to know who's who and what's what.

And then I just want to get on with it.

So if it's all right with you, I'll start with who's who.

First of all, there's me.

Name: Finbar Black.
Age: 15.
Looks: tall, dark, handsome, charming ...

Oops, sorry. I was dreaming there. I'll do that bit again.

Name: Finbar Black.
Age: 15.
Looks: normal.

That's better.

Next, my dad.

Name: Alfred Black.
Age: 35.
Looks: boring.

Third, Dad's dad, my grandad.

Name: Ronald Black.
Age: 57.
Looks: dirty, mad, sad, greedy.

And last of all, Grandad's dad, my great-grandad.

Name: Albert Black, known to everyone as Grag.
Age: nearly dead.
Looks: hard to see. Never gets out of his chair and almost never speaks.

OK. So that's who we are. The what's what and the where is easy. It's Saturday afternoon of the last week in June, and the four of us are sitting in Grandad's front room, watching TV.

The time is nearly four o'clock, and we've been sitting here since lunchtime.

I'm bored to death. From outside I can hear the summer sounds of little kids playing in the street. In the distance I can hear chimes from an ice-cream van. Hip-hop beats boom from the radio of a car near by. I can imagine the hot sun, burning down from a bright blue sky outside.

That's all outside.

In here, in this dusty old room, the curtains are shut and the outside world feels as if it's a million miles away.

There's no summer in here.

All we've got is horse-racing on the TV, a roomful of stale air, and three living corpses – Dad, Grandad and Grag. They haven't made a sound in the last half-hour apart from the odd sly fart. They never *say* anything. They just sit there – Dad and Grandad are slumped together on the sofa. Grag is in his lumpy old armchair. All three are staring blankly at the TV screen. They seem to suck the life out of everything around them.

Dragging me down.

Are they alive at all?

I wouldn't feel so bad if they weren't my own family – my own flesh and blood. But they *made* me. And every time I look at them, I wonder if that's how I'll look in years to come. Is that how I'll be in the future? Thinking like that makes me shiver. I don't want to end up like them. I don't want to be old. I don't even want to *think* about being old.

'So,' I tell myself, 'don't think about it. Think about something else.'

Like what?

'I don't know ... anything. Think about Amy –'

No, I don't want to think about her.

'Why not? Just because –'

Shut up.

Those last two words are so clear in my head that for a moment I think maybe I've said them out loud. I feel a bit embarrassed, so I look up carefully ... Did anyone notice?

It's all right – they're all still staring at the TV.

Mind you, this lot wouldn't budge if a bomb went off. They don't notice anything.

Back to Amy. She's my girlfriend ... or rather, she was my girlfriend.

In fact, I've only ever spoken to her twice. The first time was last week when I asked her to meet me at the bus stop tonight. The second time was last night when she rang me up and told me she had something better to do.

I hear myself say, "Shall we open the curtains?"

No one replies.

"Dad?" I say.

"What?" he grunts.

"Can I open the curtains?"

"No," Grandad says. He goes on staring at the TV.

"But it's a really nice day –"

"Just leave 'em," mutters Grandad.

I look at Dad.

"The sun's too bright," Dad says. "It glares on the TV screen."

"Hurts my eyes," Grandad adds.

"It hurts his eyes," Dad repeats.

"OK," I say.

And we all sink back into silence.

What am I doing here?

I always visit my dad on the last Saturday of every month. I don't want to, and I don't think he wants me to, but I've been coming here on Saturdays for so long now that we don't think about it much. It's just something that happens. It's what we do. On the last Saturday of every month, I get on a bus and rattle across town to visit my dad.

I don't have to visit him. I mean, it's not the law. My mum and dad aren't even properly divorced. They just don't live together. They haven't done for the last seven years.

I remember Mum said to Dad, "What's the point in getting a divorce? No one in their right mind is going to want to marry you, and I won't get married again for all the tea in China. Let's not waste loads of money on divorce lawyers. I'll stay here with Finbar and you can go and live with your dad. We'll leave things at that – OK?"

"But –" said Dad.

"*OK?*"

"OK."

And they didn't talk about a divorce after that at all.

It's out of habit that I'm sitting here now, at Dad's, bored stupid. I wonder how much longer I can stand it. I don't have to stay here. I can go whenever I want. I could go right now. The trouble is, I always stay for tea, and if I leave now, they'll all ask me questions –

"What's the matter, Finbar?"

"Why are you going now?"

"Where are you going?"

I don't want questions. Questions mean answers, and answers mean lies, and I can't be bothered to make up any lies.

But I don't want to stay for tea. We have tea around five o'clock, and that's almost an hour away. Then I've got to go to the chip shop, come back, dish out the chips, wait for everyone to finish, make a cup of tea, then *another* cup of tea. And then it'll be getting on for six o'clock. At last. That's when I can go.

Six o'clock?

'No way,' I'm thinking to myself. 'Six o'clock is two hours away. Two more hours of this? You must be joking. I can't sit here for another two hours. If I sit here for another two hours –'

Then –

CRASH!

"What was that?" Dad says. He looks towards the door.

"Back door," I say, standing up. "I think –"

BANG!

The sound of the back door slamming shut –

CLACK – CLACK.

And someone bolting it.

Dad turns to Grandad. "Are you expecting anyone?"

Grandad shakes his head.

And now we're all staring at the door. We're listening hard to the sound of footsteps crossing the floor and moving quickly towards us in the front room. Time seems to have frozen. No one moves. No one says anything. There isn't time. The sound of the footsteps is all there is.

Clomp, clomp, clomp.

'It's probably nothing ...' I start to think.

Then someone dressed all in black and wearing a motorbike helmet bursts through the door and points a gun at my head.

CHAPTER 2
AN EMPTY MESS

"You!" the stranger shouts, jabbing the gun at me. "Don't move ... stay there ... shut up ... sit down ..."

"Whuh?" is all I can say.

"SIT DOWN!"

I sit down.

Petrified.

Shocked.

And with no idea what to do.

The stranger is dressed all in black – black leather trousers, black leather jacket, black leather boots and a black motorbike helmet. The helmet has a tinted visor, so I can't see who's wearing it, but the voice is female – I'm sure of that. It's a woman … a girl, maybe. She's not that big. About as tall as me. Slim, but curvy, with small feet and small hands.

"What are you looking at?" she snaps.

"Nunh … nothing," I say. I look down quickly.

"What do you want?" Dad says to her. "What are you doing?"

"Shut up and sit down," she tells him, and she moves across to the window.

As Dad sits down, I look up and watch as the girl walks across the room. A small black rucksack bangs up and down on her back. She stops beside the window and stands with her back against the side wall. Then she carefully pulls back the curtain and peeks outside. A ray of sunlight cuts into the dim room and lights up clouds of floating dust.

"We haven't got any money," Dad tells her.

She drops the curtain and points the gun at him. "I told you to shut up. Is the front door locked?"

Dad doesn't answer, just looks at her.

"Are you *deaf*?" she says to him.

Dad looks at Grandad. Grandad shrugs. Dad looks at me. I shrug.

The girl says to me, "What's your name?"

"Who – me?" I answer like an idiot.

"Yes – *you*. What's your name?"

"Finbar."

"Right, Finbar," she says. "Go and check the front door. Make sure it's locked and bolted. And while you're at it, turn off the TV and shut all the windows and curtains upstairs." She's staring at me, a round black helmet-head, and I can't see her eyes. I'm staring back at her, trying to see behind the visor, trying to see what her face looks like ... but then she steps towards me and points the gun at my head, and I don't want to see anything any more.

"Get up," she says.

I get up.

"Turn off the TV."

I do it.

She waves the gun at the hall door. "Front door, windows, curtains, upstairs ... get going. NOW!"

My legs are shaking as I start to move into the hall. My head buzzes with fear.

The girl aims the gun at Dad's head and says to me, "If you're not back in two minutes, he's dead meat – OK?"

I nod my head and walk out into the hall.

This is all new to me. I haven't got a clue what to do. I could try to open the front door and run out into the street and yell for help, but that's a bit risky. This girl – whoever she is, she might not shoot Dad ... she might just be bluffing – but who knows? Maybe she's a psycho. Maybe she would shoot him just like that. Maybe she likes killing people.

'Best play safe,' I tell myself.

So I lock the front door and bolt it. Then I run upstairs and check that all the windows are closed. I know they are. No one's opened them for years – but I check anyway. Then I close all the curtains. Then I stop for a moment. I try to think if I can do anything … anything smart or clever … but my head's just an empty mess. I can't think of anything. So I run downstairs and go back into the front room.

No one's moved.

Dad, Grandad and Grag are still sitting down, and the girl in black is still standing behind them. Dad looks out of it and a little bit scared. But Grandad seems calm enough. He looks blank, cold, hard – as if he's thinking. Across the room, Grag looks the same as always – dribbly and in another world. The girl has still got the gun in her hand, and she's still got the helmet on, but she's taken the rucksack off her back and put it on the table.

"Sit down," she tells me, and she points at the chair.

I cross the room. Why is she pointing? I mean, there's only one place I can sit. I'm not going to sit on the floor, am I? But I don't say anything. I just keep quiet and sit down.

"Did you see anything?" the girl says to me.

"What do you mean?" I say.

"Did you *see* anything?"

"Where?"

"Outside ... on the street. Was there anyone there?"

"Like who?"

"Anyone," she snaps. "What's the matter with you? It's a simple question, isn't it?" She takes a deep breath, calms herself down, then asks me again. "When you were at the window ... did you see anyone outside?"

I shake my head. "I didn't look."

"Right," she says. "OK."

I can't see her from where I'm sitting. Even if I could, I wouldn't be able to see her face, but I get the feeling she doesn't know what to do next. Her voice shakes. She sounds as if she's in a panic. But she's not scared.

"Look," Dad says to her. "Why don't you just take what you want and go? We won't do anything. I promise. We won't call the police –"

"Shut up," she snaps.

He doesn't shut up. He says, "We haven't got any money, but Grag's got some old war medals upstairs and –"

"Will you SHUT UP!" the girl yells. "I don't want your bloody war medals, for God's sake. Jesus. I wouldn't take anything from this house if you paid me. I mean, look at this room." She waves the gun around. "Christ, it *stinks* in here. It smells like someone's rotting." She turns to Dad. "I don't want anything – all right? All I want is for you to shut up and let me think."

The room goes quiet. Very quiet. It's so quiet that I can hear the faint tick-tock of the clock on the mantelpiece, the tinny whirr of the cogs and springs ... and I can hear the girl behind us, pacing around ... and, from across the room, I can hear Grag's thick heavy breathing.

And then I work out that it's not only quiet in here ... it's quiet outside, as well. The kids have stopped playing. There's no traffic noise, no music, no distant ice-cream vans ... no sounds at all.

"She's on the run," Grandad says softly.

"What?" Dad says.

"She's –"

"Hey," says the girl. "What did you say?"

Grandad turns around and looks at her.
"You're on the run, aren't you? You've done
something." He looks at the rucksack on the table.
"What have you got in there?"

"Turn around," she tells him. "Don't –"

"Money?" he says. "Is it money? You've
robbed somewhere, haven't you? You've robbed
somewhere and something's gone wrong and now
you're –"

"Old man," she says coldly, "if you don't shut
your mouth and turn around now, I'm going to pull
this trigger and paint the walls with your brain.
Do you understand?"

There's a moment's silence, and then out of
the corner of my eye I see Grandad turn round
with a knowing grin on his face. He nudges Dad
with his elbow. When Dad looks at him, Grandad
winks. He rubs his thumb slyly against his fingers,

and says without making a noise – *money, money, money.*

I don't get it for a second or two. I don't understand what he means.

And then, all at once, it hits me. Money – he wants her money. I stare at him. I hope I'm wrong but I can tell by the look on his face that I'm not. The stupid old man wants her money. Can you believe it? He's sitting there, in front of a girl with a gun, and all he can think about is how to get her money.

It's crazy.

He doesn't even know if she's got any money. There might be anything in that rucksack – library books, dirty washing, sandwiches, shopping. He's only guessing she's some kind of criminal. He doesn't know she's on the run from the police. I mean, just because she's got a gun –

"ALICE MAY!"

A metallic voice blasts away the silence.

"ALICE MAY!"

A megaphone, from the street outside.

"THIS IS THE POLICE. WE KNOW YOU'RE IN THERE, ALICE! GIVE YOURSELF UP NOW. COME OUT OF THE HOUSE WITH YOUR HANDS ON YOUR HEAD."

CHAPTER 3
STUNNING

As the sound of the megaphone voice dies in the air, a weird silence takes over. Somehow, everything seems quieter than quiet. The silence is heavy and still. It hangs in the air, waiting, like an invisible cloud.

Then the girl says, "Shit!" and the spell is broken. We all turn round and look at her.

"See?" says Grandad. "I told you, didn't I? I *told* you she was on the run."

"Shut up," she spits. Then she hits the table with her fist – *bang, bang, bang* – and curses again. "Shit, shit, SHIT. How the hell do they know my name?"

"I expect it's the bike," Grandad says.

"What?"

"Did you have a motorbike?"

"*What?*"

"It's simple. You robbed some place and got away on a motorbike. Someone probably clocked the plates –"

"Clocked the plates?"

"Then called the cops and gave 'em the numbers. The cops checked their computer and got your name ... Alice May."

The girl – Alice May – stares at him. She's still got her helmet on. You can't see her face, so it's as if an alien is staring at him and you can't see its eyes. Then she starts moving towards Grandad, walking slowly, the gun in her hand. I think for a moment that she's going to kill him, she's going to put the gun to his head and kill him.

But she doesn't. She stops ... stands there for a moment, looking really hard at Grandad and then she reaches up and takes off her helmet.

Her face is stunning, pale and delicate. It looks like the face of a china doll. Her mouth is small, with small white teeth, and her eyes are emerald green. I stare at her – all goggle-eyed – and she takes off her gloves and moves her hand to the back of her neck. She unties a band, and shakes her head from side to side. I watch with my mouth open as a wave of red hair falls across her shoulders – red and shiny and perfectly straight.

"I stole the motorbike, you idiot," she sneers at Grandad. "Do you think I'd use my own bike on a job?"

Grandad shrugs.

"Not that it's got anything to do with you, anyway," she says.

"I was only trying to help," he tells her. "What did you rob? The Post Office? They're not going to have much on a Saturday –"

The megaphone voice breaks in on him.

"MISS MAY," it calls out. "THE HOUSE IS SURROUNDED WITH ARMED POLICE … THERE'S NO WAY OUT … PLEASE GIVE YOURSELF UP … LET'S FINISH THIS BEFORE IT'S TOO LATE."

Alice closes her eyes for a moment, then breathes out hard and opens them again, staring blankly at the window.

I don't want to admit it, but I can't stop looking at her. Even with all this stuff going on, I just can't stop staring at her. I mean, she's *incredible*. Soft and smooth and perfect. She looks like a film star, or a model, or a girl in an advert ...

"Hey – Finbar," she says suddenly. "Will you please stop ogling me?"

I look away and I blush.

"Christ," she says to herself, "that's all I need."

I look up. I try to look hurt, like – how dare you accuse me of ogling you, but she's already forgotten about me. Right now, as she makes her way over to the window, keeping in close to the wall, she's not thinking about me at all. And that's fine with me.

She stands with her back to the wall and she pushes the edge of the curtain with her gun. She looks out quickly. Almost at once, she jerks her head back again.

"Damn it," she whispers to herself.

"They'll have the back surrounded, too," Dad says. "You might as well give yourself up."

"You reckon?" she says, unzipping her jacket and glaring at him. Under the jacket she's wearing a short black vest. You can see a gleaming silver stud in her belly button. Before she catches me ogling again, I look away and down to the floor.

"You know they're right, don't you?" Dad says to her. "There's no way out ... even if you could get out, the cops know who you are, so they're going to know where you live." He wipes his nose on his sleeve. "Keeping us here isn't going to help. It's only going to make things worse –"

"I'll make things worse for *you* if you don't shut your mouth," she says.

"Don't be stupid –"

"Don't call *me* stupid –"

"Whoah," Grandad says. He holds up his hand to try and calm things down. "There's no need for all this," he says. He looks at Dad, then at Alice.

"Let's all calm down and talk about it. I'm sure we can –"

Then the phone rings.

We all stare at it for a second or two – *bleep, bleep … bleep, bleep … bleep, bleep.*

None of us knows what to do. I'm not sure if we don't know what to do because of what's going on now, or because the phone in this house never rings – none of us has ever heard it before.

After looking at Dad, and then Alice, and then me – and getting no help from any of us – Grandad picks it up in the end.

"Hello?" he says slowly. "Yes … yes, that's right." He glances at the window, then he licks his lips, looks at Alice, and then down at the floor. His voice gets lower. "Uh huh," he says into the phone. "Uh huh … yes … right … OK … who – me?" He looks at Alice again. "Ronald Black," he says. "Yes, that's right. What … in here, d'you mean? Well, there's me, my son –"

At which point, Alice steps over and grabs the phone off him. "Who's this?" she asks angrily into the phone. "Yeah? Maybe … what's *your* name?

Yeah? No ... hold on ... *you* listen. You listen to *me* – I'll tell you what's going to happen. You're going to keep everybody away from this house, *that's* what going to happen. Because if I see anything, any cops, anyone at all ... if I see or hear *anything* ... if I so much as feel that anything's wrong I'm going to start shooting – d'you understand? I'm not joking ... one false move and this house is a graveyard – OK? Right ... good ... yeah, that's right. No. NO! I'll tell you what I want when I'm ready – all right? Just keep away. Keep away, and no one gets hurt."

She slams the phone down. Her face is pale and she's breathing hard.

No one says anything. No one moves. The house is tense. The air is heavy with silence.

I don't know about the others, but I'm beginning to see how serious this is. I knew that before, of course, but now the shock's wearing off and I'm starting to see things as they really are.

And they don't look good.

We're hostages.

We're trapped in this house with someone who's scared and has a gun. She's just said she might kill us all.

We're surrounded by armed police.

Nope ... things don't look too good at all.

But you know what they say. Just when you think things can't get any worse, they do.

Grag starts it off. We're all sitting there – apart from Alice, who's standing there – and we're all waiting to see what happens, when Grag starts grumbling and groaning and getting up out of his chair.

"Hey," says Alice, pointing the gun at him. "Hey, you ... sit down. I said sit *down*."

Grag, of course, ignores her. He's stone deaf and even if he wasn't, I expect he wouldn't understand what she was saying. So he just carries on pulling himself out of his chair, grunting and dribbling like a skinny old monster wearing a cardigan.

Alice looks angry now. She glares at him for a second, and then she starts moving towards him, pointing the gun at his head.

"I told you," she snarls. "I told you."

But as she gets closer to Grag, and sees how old and shaky he is, her anger seems to go. She walks more slowly, she lowers the gun, and she doesn't seem so sure of herself.

"What's he doing?" she says in a worried voice. "Make him sit down."

"It's all right," Dad tells her. "He's not doing anything. He just needs to go to the toilet."

"Well, he can't," says Alice, watching Grag, who's still trying to get out of his chair. "Tell him to sit down."

"Best let him go," Grandad says with a chuckle, "unless you want to get gassed."

Alice looks around and scowls at Grandad. "You think this is funny?" Then she looks back at Grag again. "What's wrong with him?" she says.

"He's old," Dad tells her.

"Been old for years," adds Grandad. "He's been old for so long his brain's given up. Can't control himself most of the time." Grag lets out a weedy little fart. "See?" Grandad grins. "Look, I'd better take him to the bathroom –"

"No," says Alice, turning around. "No one leaves this room."

"He's got to go," Grandad says. "Look at him. If I don't get him upstairs soon, he's going to have an accident. You don't want that, do you?"

Alice doesn't know what she wants. She looks at Grandad, then wrinkles her nose and looks across at Grag. He's standing up now, but he's bent over, fiddling with the zip of his trousers.

"Come on," Grandad pleads. "Let me take him to the bathroom. I won't do anything. I won't try to escape or anything. I give you my word. I'll just take him to the toilet, let him do his stuff, and then I'll bring him right back down again. Trust me – I'm not going to run out on my own family, am I?"

Me and Dad look at each other. We both know that Grandad is well able to run out on his own family. He's done it once already, 30 years ago, when Dad was just a kid. He won't feel bad about doing it again.

In the end Alice says, "All right. Get him upstairs, but be quick. And if you don't come back, or if you do anything stupid ..." She turns the gun on me. "The kid gets it first – OK?"

Grandad nods, then gets up and goes over to Grag and starts helping him out of the room.

As they shuffle out, I wonder if I'll ever see them again.

CHAPTER 4
JAMES BOND

Now it's just the three of us – me and Dad sitting down, with Alice standing behind us. I look across at Dad. He's staring at nothing, his eyes unblinking, his hands perfectly still in his lap. Is he thinking about anything at all?

I'm still thinking about Grandad and wondering what he's doing. I know he's up to something, because he *never* takes Grag to the bathroom. Come to think of it, he never does anything for Grag. He must be up to something and if it doesn't work out, I'll end up paying for it.

Bang bang – bye bye, Finbar.

Then I hear Dad say, "Why don't you sit down for a minute? Try to relax?"

"Relax?" says Alice. "You want me to *relax*?"

"Why not?" Dad says. "It can't hurt, can it? The cops aren't going to do anything for a while. They're not in any hurry."

Alice doesn't answer. Instead, she starts walking about behind us – up and down, up and down, up and down ...

"You're wearing out the carpet," Dad tells her.

Alice stops.

"Don't you ever shut up?" she says.

Dad grins. "It was the Co-op, wasn't it?"

"What?" Alice says.

"The Co-op ... you robbed the Co-op."

She walks round the sofa and stands in front of him. "How do you know that?"

Dad grins again. "You used to work there – on the check-out."

She stares at him. She doesn't know what to say.

"Your hair was different then," he says, "but I remember you. You drove a motorbike. You used to park it round the back. I haven't seen you there for a couple of months, so I guess you left, or were asked to leave ..."

'Yeah,' I'm thinking to myself. 'Yeah, I remember her now. She had short blonde hair, kind of curly at the back, and she used to wear lots of make-up, and she hardly ever smiled or said hello and she never helped you to pack your bags.'

"That's how they know who you are," Dad is telling her. "One of the staff must have recognised you."

Alice shakes her head. "How? I had all this gear on. No one could see my face, I was wearing gloves, it wasn't my bike ..."

Dad shrugs. "There's lots of ways of knowing who people are – the way they walk, the sound of their voice, their shape ..." He looks at her. "You can't hide everything."

She looks at him closely, and just for a second, I think she's going to hit Dad. But then Grandad is suddenly there, in the doorway, and we all turn to look at him – and my heart sinks down to the ground.

He's standing there with a gun in his hand.

I can't believe it.

I blink and look again, just to make sure I'm not seeing things – but I'm not. He's standing there like some kind of super-cop – legs apart, arms stretched out in front, both hands gripping the gun, pointing it at Alice's head.

"Drop it," he tells her. "Drop your gun, now."

She just looks at him.

So does Dad.

And so do I.

I'm sure we're all thinking the same thing – what the hell is he doing? He's going to get us all killed. I mean, who does he think he is – James Bond?

There's a long silence.

I keep on looking at the gun in Grandad's hand. I've seen it before. It's Grag's old army pistol. He keeps it in a box full of rubbish in his room. It's a huge old gun with a very long barrel ... all rusty and black and crappy. Grag showed it to me once. I could hardly pick it up – it weighs a ton.

But Grandad seems OK with it. He aims it steadily at Alice's head as he takes a couple of steps forward and comes into the room.

"Are you *deaf?*" he says to her. "I told you – drop the gun."

She doesn't move an inch. Doesn't drop the gun. Just carries on staring at Grandad.

"This is mad," she says. "You're not going to shoot me."

"No?" Grandad says, stepping closer.

She slowly raises her gun. "No."

Now they're both standing there. They're both pointing their guns at each other, both waiting for the other one to say something.

Grandad goes first. "How much did you take?"

"That's none of your business," Alice replies.

Grandad grins. "Oh, I think it is." He cocks the gun. "*This* makes it my business. Now, how much did you get?"

"Not enough for you," she says.

"How much?"

She looks into his eyes. She doesn't say anything for a moment. Then she takes a deep breath and slowly lets it out. "Whatever I've got is mine," she says. "I need it ... my daughter needs it."

"Your daughter?" Grandad sniffs. "What's your daughter got do with it?"

"Everything." Alice's voice starts to shake. "She's got *everything* to do with it. She's why I did it, for God's sake." She angrily wipes a tear from her eye. "She's ill, OK? She needs an operation ... but they can't ... I need the money to pay for ..." Her lips start to tremble and her voice trails away. Tears run down her face. She wipes them away, takes another deep breath and tries hard to control herself.

"Ah, what's the point?" she says at last. "You won't understand ... you're a *man*. None of you understand."

Grandad stays where he is. He doesn't say anything. He doesn't put the gun down.

I can see him thinking about it all, trying to work out what to do. I don't think he cares about Alice's daughter – he doesn't care very much about anyone – but I think seeing Alice cry has confused him. Alice is right – he doesn't understand. But I don't think that matters to him.

So, without thinking, I open my mouth and say, "The gun's not loaded."

Dad snaps his head round to look at me. I can feel him staring at me, but Alice and Grandad don't move. They stay where they are, staring hard at each other. Then – without moving – Alice says to me, "What did you say?"

"Grandad's gun," I tell her. "It's not loaded."

"Shut up, you little –" Grandad starts to say.

"Are you sure?" Alice asks me.

"Don't you say another word," Grandad growls. "Don't you dare –"

"It's Grag's old army pistol," I explain. "There aren't any bullets –"

"He's lying," says Grandad. "He doesn't know –"

"The chamber's all rusted up, anyway," I say. "It's full of grunge and muck. Even if there were any bullets, you'd never be able to load them."

"Is that right?" Alice says, moving towards Grandad.

The pistol's starting to shake in his hands. "Don't come any closer," he tells her. "Stay where you are. I'm warning you ..."

"Go on, then," she says. "Shoot me. If the gun's loaded – prove it." She thrusts her head forward, as if it was a target. "Go on – shoot me."

Grandad's finger pulls on the trigger, and even though I know the gun's not loaded, I'm scared to death. What if I'm wrong? What if it *is* loaded? Anything's possible ...

Then, just as I'm thinking about the *crack* of a gunshot, Grandad's face breaks into a smile and he starts to laugh.

CHAPTER 5
BLACK HEAT

I always knew that Grandad was mad, but I never knew he was *this* mad.

Alice has her gun aimed right at his head and he's just standing there. He laughs like a maniac. I've never heard him laugh like this before, and it feels weird, and a little bit scary. Alice can't work out what to do. She's just standing there, staring at him. I don't blame her. I wouldn't know what to do, either.

"All right," she tells him. "All right ... that's enough. Shut up and put the gun down."

Grandad looks at the pistol in his hand, as if he doesn't know how it got there. Then he starts laughing again, even harder this time.

"What?" Alice says. "What's so funny?"

"Nothing," barks Grandad between laughs, "nothing at all."

"Yeah? So how come you're wetting your pants about it?"

For some reason, Grandad finds this really funny, and now he lets rip, hooting and cackling until his face is so red it looks like he's about to explode. Grag's pistol is still dangling from his hand, and Alice is watching it carefully. Her eyes are getting cold now – she's bored of waiting.

"I'm not going to tell you again," she says with menace. "Put ... the gun ... down."

"What – this?" Grandad laughs, waggling the pistol in front of her face. "You want me to put this down? Why? What are you going to do if I don't? What are you going to do, Miss May? Shoot me? *Kill* me? I don't think so –"

A sudden dull CRACK! splits the air, and Grandad's words are lost to the heart-stopping sound of a gunshot. A jagged echo freezes the room, and for a moment all I can feel is a painful ringing in my ears and a bitter smell in my nostrils ... a shocking smell of black heat and death and burnt powder.

Then my head clears and I can see Alice May pointing the gun at the ceiling, her red hair covered in scraps of plaster. I can see Grandad too. He stands, staring at her with shocked eyes and a deathly white face.

I realise I've been holding my breath for the last 20 seconds, and now it's starting to hurt, so I open my mouth and let it all out.

"*God*," Dad says to Alice. "What did you do that for?" He looks over at Grandad. "Are you all right?"

Grandad nods. He doesn't say a word.

Dad looks at me.

"I'm OK," I tell him.

He goes on looking at me.

"What?" I say.

"You snake," he says nastily.

"What do you mean?"

"You *know* what I mean –"

"All right," says Alice. "That's enough. Settle down. No one's hurt." She turns to Grandad. "Have you finished laughing now?"

Grandad nods again.

"Give me that," she says, pointing to his gun.

He passes it over without a word.

She starts to check it, opening it up and looking inside – and then the phone rings again.

Dad goes to pick it up, but Alice snatches it from him.

"Yeah?" she says. A second's silence, then, "No, it was nothing – just a warning. No, no one's hurt ... yeah, well you'll just have to trust me, won't you? No ... no, I said I'll tell you what I want when I'm ready ... no, I'm *not* ready yet ... I don't know ... listen ... all right, give me an hour ... ring me again in an hour. Any earlier, and the next shot won't go in the ceiling."

She gives the phone to Dad and tells him to hang up. He looks at her for a second, then does as he's told.

Nothing much happens for the next five minutes. We all just stay where we are. We don't say much, we don't do much. We're just waiting and thinking, thinking and waiting, waiting and thinking.

The room falls into that heavy silence again. I can hear the faint tick-tock of the clock on the mantelpiece, the tinny whirr of the cogs and springs ... I can hear the hush of the street outside. I can see clouds of dust floating in the dim light.

And everything feels weird.

Of course.

Everything's going to feel weird, isn't it? But there's something else ... something as well as the weirdness, and that's what I can feel. I don't know what I can feel. I can't explain it. But there's a new feeling ... a feeling that everything's changing.

Everything – the air, the house, the room ... me and Dad, Alice and Grandad, the things we all want, or don't want, and the way we're all thinking about each other.

I don't know. Maybe it's just me?

But, look –

There's Alice, sitting at the table, fiddling with the buckles of her rucksack. What's she thinking about? Her daughter? The police? How to get out of here without getting killed? And what does she think of me? Does she hate me for ogling her? Or is she glad that I told her about Grag's gun?

Then there's Dad and Grandad, slumped together on the sofa, staring at the blank TV screen – Dad's deep in thought, Grandad's trying to calm down again. I know what they think of me. I can tell by the dirty looks they're giving me. I'm a snake, a grass, a traitor. I've let the family down.

I'm stuck in the middle, all on my own. I don't know who I belong to, or which side I'm on, or why or how or where or when or what or whatever.

And I don't really care.

All I want to do is get out of here.

Get out of this house.

And go home.

CHAPTER 6
A DEAL

Everything's quiet for another five minutes, and then we all get a shock when all at once there's a gushing noise from upstairs.

"What's that?" Alice hisses, jumping to her feet.

"That's Grag." Dad grins. "Flushing the toilet."

"Shit," Alice says. "I forgot all about him."

"Easy to do," Grandad says.

Alice looks at him, and sees that he's back to normal. He's not mad or scared any more, he's just Grandad.

"He's your father," Alice says.

"So?"

"You ought to show him some respect."

"Why?"

"Because he's your *father* ... you're his son."

Grandad shrugs. "I didn't ask to be born."

Alice opens her mouth, but she can't think of anything to say, so she just shakes her head.

Grandad grins at her. "Let's talk."

"I'm not talking to you ... there's nothing to talk about."

"What about your daughter?"

"What about her?"

"Well," says Grandad, "you're not going to be much help to her when you're in prison, are you? No mummy, no money, no operation, no daughter –"

"God," spits Alice. "You really are *disgusting*, aren't you?"

"Maybe," Grandad admits. "But I'm right, aren't I? I mean, if you get out of here, you'll go to prison for sure. Then there'll be no money or mummy for your daughter. She'll get taken into care –"

"No!"

"And that's the best that can happen. The worst ... well, let's not think about the worst, shall we?" He puts his finger to his head and mimes a gunshot. "Pow!" he says. "Armed robber, Alice May, mother of a sickly child, killed by police in a hostage situation ..."

Alice glares at him.

He looks back, grinning.

And I'm thinking, 'Well, you have to admit, he's got a point, hasn't he? It's hard to accept, I know, but he's got a point there.'

"All right," Alice says to him. "What are you trying to say?"

Grandad looks at her, enjoying himself, then says, "You want to get out of here?"

"Stupid question," she replies.

He looks at her.

"Yes," she sighs. "Yes, I want to get out of here."

"OK," he says. "So, what's it worth?"

"What's it worth? What do you mean?"

"I mean – what's it worth? How much will you pay to get out of here? That's what I mean."

"You can get me out?"

"Maybe."

"What about the police?"

"I can get you out."

"How?"

Grandad just smiles.

And for the next few seconds I can feel the silence, a storm of thoughts, pulsing in the air.

Grandad's waiting, hiding his plans.

Dad's giving nothing away.

And Alice is thinking, thinking hard ... Is it a trap? A trick? A lie? A game? Is it worth taking the risk?

I don't think she's got much to lose.

"Yes or No?" Grandad says, looking up at the clock. "It's up to you, Alice. Make up your mind. But don't take too long ... the cops won't wait for ever."

Alice looks at him. "How much do you want?"

He smiles. "How much have you got?"

Her eyes flick over to the rucksack on the table. "Look," she says, "it's not much –"

"How much?"

She wipes some sweat from her brow and then she moves across to the table. "Make me an offer," she says.

Grandad laughs. "What do you think this is – a car-boot sale?"

"All right," says Alice. "Ten per cent."

"Of what?" says Dad.

She looks at him. "Of what I've got."

"Half," Dad says.

"Half? No way."

"Take it or leave it," Grandad says.

"I'll leave it, then."

"You'll end up with nothing."

"So will you."

Grandad and Dad look at each other. Alice watches them. Dad leans over and whispers something in Grandad's ear. Grandad listens. He looks at Alice. Then he looks at Dad. Then he nods his head.

"30 per cent," Dad says to Alice.

"20," Alice replies.

"Each?"

Now Alice looks at me, and – like a fool – I smile at her. God knows why. I mean, she's not looking for smiles, is she? But she smiles back at me – cool and calm and oh so pretty – and I feel my face burning up. I'm blushing right to the tips of my ears.

But I don't mind.

I don't mind at all.

And then she winks at me, and my heart sings. She turns and says to Dad, "When you say each, what do you mean?"

"20 per cent for me, 20 per cent for him," he says, pointing to Grandad.

Alice nods. "What about Finbar?"

"What about him?" Dad snorts, like I'm not part of this, like I'm nothing.

"He's your son," Alice says. "I just thought –"

"If you want to give him something, that's up to you," Dad says. "But it comes out of your share, not ours – all right?"

"OK," says Alice. "But you're not getting 20 per cent each. I'll give you a third between you, and that's it. No more haggling. That's 33 per cent. Last offer."

Dad and Grandad start talking to each other, whispering and mumbling like a couple of people in a quiz show.

I don't know what to do, or where to look. I'm still feeling embarrassed about smiling at Alice, but now I'm feeling embarrassed about Dad, too. I'm used to him, so it doesn't bother me when he treats me like crap, but when he does it in front of someone else ... Well, I just can't help feeling really bad. Not for me, but for him.

I sit there staring at the floor, listening to Dad and Grandad's whispering, until at last the whispering stops and Grandad looks up and says, "All right, Miss May – you've got yourself a deal."

CHAPTER 7
THE CLEVER PART

It's hard to keep track of the time when weird things are happening. The seconds and minutes seem to speed up and slow down ... speed up, slow down ... faster, slower ... faster, slower.

Right now – as Dad and Grandad sit at the table, discussing their plan with Alice – it feels like a month ago that Alice was talking to the cops on the phone, telling them to ring her back in an hour. But, at the same time, it feels as if it was only five minutes ago. A month or five minutes? In here, right now, they both feel the same – a month *is* five minutes, and five minutes *is* a month. I think the phone call was about half an hour ago, but I've lost touch with the real world.

As I said, Dad and Grandad are sitting at the table, discussing their plan with Alice.

From where I am – still sitting in the armchair – it's an odd scene. Alice is sitting on one side of the table, with the rucksack on her knee and the gun in her hand. Dad and Grandad are sitting side by side across the table from her and watching everything she does. They're watching her, she's watching them … watching her … watching them. They're all looking edgy. They don't know what to do with their hands and they're all trying to stay cool. Talking calmly, coldly, keeping things practical.

"I need to be sure," Alice says. "I need to know you'll keep your side of the deal. I'm not giving you any money until I know what I'm getting."

"Look," Grandad says, "we haven't got time to mess around."

"So – tell me how you're going to get me out of here."

"If we tell you, what's to stop you keeping all the money?"

"I don't know, do I? I don't know what your plans are. How can I plan to cheat you when I don't even know what you're going to do?"

"Eh?" Grandad says, scratching his head.

"You don't have to tell me everything," Alice says. "You don't have to give me all the details ... just give me an idea of how I'm going to get out of here. Then, if it sounds OK, we can start working out the money."

Grandad looks at Dad to see what he thinks.

Dad nods. "All right," he says after a while. "Tell her. But keep the details to yourself."

Grandad waits for a moment, working out what to say and what to leave out. Then he turns to Alice and starts to explain. "OK," he says. "Well, there's this place in the attic, a hiding place –"

"Is that all?" Alice says with a laugh. "A hiding place in the attic?"

"No," Grandad sneers, "that's not *all*. If you'll just let me finish."

"Go on, then," says Alice.

Grandad sighs, shakes his head, then goes on. "Right, well, as I was saying, there's a hiding place in the attic, but that's not the clever part. The clever part is the walls."

"The walls?" Alice says.

"Yeah," Grandad says, and his eyes light up. "You see, on these old streets, the houses were built with shared attics. Most of 'em have been divided now, but the walls that have been put up are only plasterboard, so all you've got to do is give 'em a good kick and you're into the attic next door." He sniffs hard and scratches his head. "So, what we do is ... we take you up into the attic, kick a hole through the dividing wall. Then you can go through into the attic of the house next door. There's a hatch down from the attic. You can open that, let down the ladder and – bingo! – you're into the house next door. The neighbours are in Spain at the moment, so the house is empty. But it doesn't matter, because you won't go down there anyway. You'll tuck yourself away in the hiding place." He grins, looking pleased with himself. "See? Do you get it now?"

Alice frowns. "No, not really."

Grandad frowns back at her, then looks at Dad. "Did I leave out too much?"

"Not really," Dad says. He turns to Alice and says, "Look, it's simple – when the police ring up, we tell them you ran off into the attic. They come in, go up into the attic, and when they see the hole in the wall, and the open hatch next door and the ladder, they'll think you've escaped through the house next door."

Alice nods. "But, in fact, I'm still hiding in *your* attic."

"Right," Dad says.

"And then what?"

"Then," Dad says, "the cops'll hang around for a while – checking for prints, asking questions, taking statements, that kind of stuff – and then, in the end, they'll go."

"And then I come down," Alice says.

"Right."

"And sneak off into the darkness."

"Right."

She looks across at me. It's only a tiny glance, but I can see she's thinking about the plan, and if it will work. It's as if she's saying, "What do you think? I mean, it sounds OK, doesn't it? But I don't trust these old guys. I don't trust them one bit ..."

Maybe I'm wrong. Maybe she's just looking at me for something to do? Like I'm a crappy old photo or something.

Dad says to her, "So ... what do you think?"

She turns back to him. "This hiding place," she says. "How big is it? I mean, I'm going to be stuck up there for a long time. Will I have enough room to breathe?"

"It's big enough," Grandad says. "You can stand up, move around a bit. We'll give you some water. You'll be OK."

"Right," Alice says. "How's the money going to work?"

"You give us our share before you go up, and take the rest with you."

"No way." Alice shakes her head. "You think I'm stupid? Once you've got your share, you'll tell the cops where I am –"

"Of course we won't," says Dad. "If we tell them where you are, you'll tell them you gave us the money, and that we hid you, and then we'll get arrested too."

"No," Alice says. "I'll take all the money with me, and I'll give you your share when the cops have gone."

Grandad laughs.

"What?" Alice says.

"You've got a gun," he tells her. "Once the cops have gone, you're not going to give us anything, are you? I mean, do you expect us to trust you?" He looks at her, his eyes all round, and then he starts to laugh again. It doesn't sound as mad as before, but it's still not normal.

Dad doesn't seem too bothered. He just sits there, blank, staring at Alice, while Grandad hoots and splutters. Alice does her best to put up with it, staring back at him, taking no notice of Grandad's mad laugh. But, in the end, she can't take any more. She leans across the table, and jabs the gun into Grandad's head.

"No more," she says.

Grandad stops laughing – just like that. One second he's out of control, cackling like crazy, and the next second he's perfectly normal again.

"Do it again," Alice tells him, "and you'll be laughing in Hell."

He nods.

"We're running out of time," she says. "Let's get this job sorted."

For the next ten minutes they talk about money, trying to agree how to share it out without anyone cheating. Alice offers this, Dad offers that, then Grandad says something else ... but they can't agree on anything and it's getting very boring.

After a time I can't be bothered to listen any more. I start drifting off, losing myself inside my head, letting my thoughts take over.

Thoughts like –

I'm hungry.

I need to go to the toilet.

I wonder what the cops are doing?

Do they know the house next door is empty?

I wonder how old Alice is?

She doesn't look very old ... 17, 18, maybe.

I wonder how old her daughter is?

I wonder if she's married?

I wonder if she's hot in those black leather trousers?

I wonder ...

I wonder ...

I wonder ...

I wonder why Dad's standing in front of me.

CHAPTER 8
INSURANCE

"Come on," Dad says to me. "We haven't got all day."

I look up at him. He's standing right in front of me, holding a bunch of cash in his hand. His eyes are greedy and he wants to get moving.

"Come *on*," he says. "Let's go."

"Where?" I say.

He looks at me like I'm an idiot. "Haven't you been listening?"

"No," I tell him, looking around.

At the table, Alice is scooping piles of cash into her rucksack, slinging it over her shoulder, then picking up her crash helmet and a plastic

Coke bottle filled with water. Grandad is standing to one side, watching her. He's got money in his hands, too.

Dad grabs my arm and pulls me to my feet. "Let's go," he hisses. "Move!"

Then he leads me out into the hall and pushes me towards the stairs. I look back. Why are Alice and Grandad following us?

"What –" I start to say.

"You're going into the attic with her. Into the hidey-hole," Dad explains.

"Why?"

"Just shut up and listen, will you? She wants some insurance – OK? She's given us this," he says and waves some cash in my face, "and she wants to make sure we don't tell the cops where she is. You're her insurance."

We're half way up the stairs now, and Dad is breathing hard. I'm not sure if he's out of breath or just excited.

"Insurance?" I ask.

"Don't worry about it," he says. "All you've got to do is stay with her till the cops have gone. Nothing's going to happen."

"Yeah, but I don't understand. What kind of insurance?"

"Life insurance." Grandad laughs.

I turn around and look at him. He's right behind us on the stairs, with Alice right behind him. His frail old body is bent over and creaky, and he's breathing even harder than Dad, but his eyes are alive with a mad black light that fills him with energy and scares me to death. A cruel grin cracks his mouth, and he says to me, "Like your dad said, there's nothing to worry about. As long as we keep our side of the deal, you won't get hurt." He looks back at Alice. "That's right, isn't it?" he says. "You'll only kill him if we tell the police where you are."

Alice doesn't answer. She doesn't look at me.

"Hey," Grandad says with a grin at me. "Don't look like that – it was your dad's idea."

We're at the top of the stairs, now. Dad stands next to me on the landing. He leans against the wall to get his breath back. He smells hot and sweaty. I'm not sure I want to look at him ... but I have to. I have to know the truth.

"Dad?" I say.

He won't look at me.

"Is it true, Dad? *Was* it your idea?"

He wipes his sweaty face and takes my arm. "Come on – there isn't time."

"No," I tell him. "I want to know –"

"Just leave it," he snaps, pushing me along the landing. "Go on ... get moving."

The push isn't hard, but it knocks me off balance a bit. For a second I'm bursting with anger – hot and mad and crazy as hell. Then my back brushes against the wall and I find my footing again. The heat of my anger turns very cold and I don't care any more ... I don't want to know.

I just don't care.

"I need to use the toilet," I tell Dad.

He's getting the attic ladder now, pulling it down. "Go on, then," he says. "And hurry up. We haven't got all day."

I walk slowly to the bathroom, open the door – and stop at the sight of Grag. He's standing there, with his trousers round his ankles, staring at the wall.

"Are you all right?" I ask him.

He turns his head and looks at me, his eyes dim and his mouth hanging open.

"Chips," he says.

"Yeah," I tell him. "I know."

I get his trousers done up and gently take him out onto the landing. Then I shut the door and use the toilet. As I stare at the wall, my head feels empty. Nothing seems real any more. I flush the toilet, wash my hands, then go back out to the landing. The attic ladder is down and Dad is climbing up.

"What are you waiting for?" Grandad says. He's standing at the foot of the ladder. "Get up there."

I look at him for a moment, then climb the ladder into the attic.

It's a big old place, dimly lit by a naked light bulb which hangs from a rafter. Rubbish is piled up everywhere – boxes, bin bags, broken-up chairs, heaps of old books and faded magazines. Everything is covered with dust and soot.

Alice is standing by an old wardrobe that's propped against the chimney stack. Dad kicks a hole through the wall into the attic next door. It doesn't take long. *Boot, boot, boot* and the plasterboard breaks. Dad grabs an edge of it and rips out a dirty great chunk. He leaves a hole in the wall that's big enough to climb through. He gets through the hole in a flash, into the attic next door, and then he bends down and opens their hatch.

'If the police are down there,' I think, 'you've had it.'

What would it be like? The sudden crack of a rifle, Dad flying backwards, shot in the face. I wonder how I'd feel. Good? Bad? Happy? Sad?

I don't know and it doesn't matter, because it doesn't happen. Dad opens the hatch, peers through the hole, lets down their ladder and then scurries back through the hole into our attic.

"Right," he says, dripping with sweat. "Are you two ready?"

Without saying a word, I walk over to the wardrobe where Alice is standing. It's a big one – tall and wide with double doors. I remember it from my childhood. I don't remember where it came from, but I do know I used to get inside it sometimes, shut the doors and hide away in the darkness.

"Finbar," Dad says.

"What?"

"Wake up."

He opens the wardrobe doors. Alice steps up and starts to go inside, but Dad holds her back and steps inside himself. I know what he's doing, but Alice doesn't. She watches him, trying to work out what he's up to.

Dad pulls a rusty screw on the back wall of the wardrobe. The back wall creaks and then opens up to reveal the inside of the chimney stack. It looks like a little brick room – blackened brick walls, a narrow, dusty brick floor. A pale ray of daylight shines down through the chimney.

Alice lets out a low whistle. "Not bad," she says. "Not bad at all."

"Yeah," Dad says, stepping out. "Once you're inside, I'll throw some junk in the wardrobe, just in case the cops take a look. But I don't think they will. As soon as they see the attic next door, they won't bother looking up here. All you've got to do is stay inside until I let you out, and keep your mouth shut. That's all. Keep your mouth shut, and everything will be all right. Understand?"

Alice nods.

I don't do anything.

"OK," says Dad. "In you go, then."

Alice looks at me, then she steps into the wardrobe and goes through into the chimney stack. As she stands there checking things out, looking around at the walls and the floor, with her red hair shining in the half-light, a weird thought flashes through my mind.

I can see that everything depends on what I do next – go inside, or don't go inside. If I go inside, I'll become one thing. If I stay here, I'll become another. It's all up to me. Go inside, don't go inside. Different choice, different future, different history.

I suppose if I had enough time or energy, it might be worth having a think about it ... but I don't have enough time. I step through the wardrobe and join Alice May in the chimney stack.

CHAPTER 9
TWO OF US

Now there's just the two of us – Alice sitting at one end of the little brick room, and me sitting at the other. It's small, and the air's dusty and stale. The summer heat makes it feel as if we're stuck in an oven. But it's not too bad. There's just enough room to stretch out our legs without touching each other, and the heat's just about OK if we don't move. There's enough light to see who we're talking to. Not that we're talking that much. In fact, since Dad closed the doors about five minutes ago, we've haven't said a single word to each other. Alice is too busy listening. Listening as Dad fills the wardrobe with junk, then shuts the outer doors, then walks off across the attic, down the ladder and back downstairs. Now she's listening for the phone ... listening hard ... her eyes closed tight.

73

"You won't hear it from up here," I tell her.

She opens her eyes. "What?"

"The phone – you won't hear it from up here."

She looks at me for a long time, then looks away and starts shifting around – wiggling her bum around, stretching her neck, moving her legs – until finally she settles down with her arms resting on her propped-up knees, and her back against the wall. The little black rucksack is lying on the floor between her legs. She reaches inside, pulls out the plastic bottle and takes a long drink. Water spills from her mouth, dripping down her chin, making her vest wet. She offers me the bottle. I shake my head. She wipes her mouth and puts the bottle on the floor, then takes the pistol out of her pocket and rests it on top of the rucksack. Finally, she pulls the rucksack in closer to her body. She leans back and looks at me.

"So," she says. "What do you think, Finbar?"

"About what?"

"This," she says, looking around. "All this. Stuck in a chimney, waiting for the cops …" She smiles at me. "I bet you didn't think you'd be spending your Saturday night like *this*, did you?"

"Not really."

"Well," she says. "I'm sorry if I messed up your plans."

"That's all right."

"What were they, anyway? I mean, if you weren't stuck in here, what would you be doing?"

'I'd be at home,' I think, 'with my mum, watching Saturday-night crap on the telly.'

But I don't tell her that, do I? Instead, I say, "I was going to meet my girlfriend. We were going to a club."

"Really? Sounds great."

"Yeah."

"What's her name?"

"Who?"

"Your *girlfriend*."

"Oh, right. Amy ... she's called Amy."

Alice nods, her green eyes twinkling in the dim light. "Is she pretty, this Amy?"

"She's all right."

"Just 'all right'?"

"Yeah, she's pretty."

"What's she going to do when you don't turn up? Is she going to dump you, d'you think?"

"I don't know …"

"I'm sure she'll understand when you tell her what happened." Alice smiles. "Tell her you spent the night in a chimney stack with a red-headed girl dressed in leather – *of course*, she'll understand."

"Yeah …"

"That's a joke, Finbar. I'm trying to lighten things up, here."

"I know."

She gives me that look again, staring hard into my eyes. I don't know what to do. I don't know how to feel … about Alice, about myself, about anything. I don't know what's going on here.

"Look," she says, "I'm sorry – OK? I didn't mean to get you into all this. It just happened. I wish there was something I could do about it, but there isn't. All I can do is say sorry. So ... you know ... I'm sorry. All right?"

"Yeah," I tell her.

She bends her head down and looks at me. "You sure?"

"Yeah, it's OK ... honestly."

"Good." She wipes some soot from her hands and looks up through the chimney. "What is this place, anyway? I mean, how come your crazy old grandad's got a hiding place in his chimney?"

"He used to buy and sell things," I tell her. "Sometimes they were the kind of things he had to hide. So he built himself this place."

"What?" She grins. "You mean stolen stuff?"

"I suppose so ... yeah."

"Well, well, well." She laughs softly. "That explains a lot." She looks at me. "You know he's totally mad, don't you?"

"Yeah."

"It doesn't run in the family, does it? I mean, you're not going to go mental on me, are you?"

"Not if I can help it."

She nods and grins, then rubs her neck, closes her eyes, and yawns.

'She must be tired,' I think. 'Tired and hungry.'

I watch her as she lowers her head and rests it on her knees, and then I listen to the silence – the wood creaking, the whisper of a breeze, the distant cheeping of birds.

'Take the gun,' a voice in my head tells me.

What?

'The gun ... on her bag ... take it now, while she's not looking.'

Then what?

'I don't know ...'

What am I going to do with a gun?

Alice stirs, lets out a sigh, then lifts her head and looks at me. For a moment she doesn't know where she is or what's going on. Then it all comes back to her. She stretches and says, "How long do you think it'll be before the cops get here?"

"I don't know ... not long, I suppose."

"I expect your dad and grandad will try something, don't you think?"

"Like what?"

"I don't know," she says with a shrug. "Something sneaky." She pats the rucksack between her legs. "They want what I've got in here – the rest of the money. They'll do whatever it takes to get it."

I look at her. "So why did you say you'd come up here?"

"I didn't have much choice, did I? Anyway, there's just a chance that it might work. It's not much of a chance, but not much is better than nothing." She grins at me. "What do you think? Do you think we've got a chance? Do you think this'll work?"

"I don't know ... maybe." I look at her. "What are you going to do if it doesn't?"

"Get arrested."

"What about me?"

"What do you mean?"

"You know ... if Dad and Grandad tell the police where we are."

She frowns at me. She doesn't understand.

"Insurance," I explain. "I'm your insurance –"

"Oh, *that*," she says. "Christ, Finbar, you didn't believe that, did you? I was bluffing. I'm not going to shoot you, for God's sake. What kind of girl do you think I am?"

"Well, I don't know. I mean ..."

"If I didn't have you with me, your dad and your grandad would give me up to the cops right away. They'd hide the money, turn me in, and that'd be that. But they're not going to do that while I've got you, are they?" She leans over and pats my leg. "You're my free ticket out of here, Finbar."

"Not free, exactly," I correct her.

"No?"

"Well, you gave Dad and Grandad a third of the money."

She smiles. "Do you really think I'm going to let them keep it?"

"But ..."

"It's mine," she says grimly. "I stole it, I took all the risks ... I'm not letting a couple of old farts take my money." Her face softens. "Don't worry, I won't hurt them. Once the cops have gone, I'll just take my money and go."

"They'll hide it away –"

"I'll find it."

"What about your daughter?"

She doesn't answer at once. She just looks at me, and the air goes cold, the walls around us seem to shrink. I've been trying not to talk about her daughter. But there's something ... something bugging me, something niggling away in my head for so long that I can't keep quiet any longer.

"My daughter?" says Alice.

"Yeah. I mean, how are you going to get her back?"

"What?"

"The police will have her, won't they? They know who you are, they know where you live. They'll have found out where your daughter is, and now they'll have her in care somewhere. So even if you do get out of here with all the money, you'll still have to get her back before you can sort out the operation she needs ..."

My voice trails off at the sight of Alice's face. She's grinning at me, her head shaking slightly, her eyes cold and bright.

"What?" I ask her. "What?"

"I haven't got a daughter, you idiot. Why would I want a *daughter*?"

"But ... but you said ..."

"God," she snorts. "You're as bad as the other two. You believe anything!"

"You haven't got a daughter?"

"Of course not. It was a story, that's all. I was playing for time ... looking for sympathy." Her voice takes on a mocking tone. "Poor little girl, needs an operation ... boo hoo hoo ..." She laughs. "Grow up, Finbar – this isn't *The Jeremy Kyle Show*. This is reality. I'm a thief. The Co-op sacked me for fiddling the till ... so I went back and robbed them. I'm a thief, that's all. Simple as that."

I'm speechless. Dumb. Empty. I just sit here, listening to all this, and a thousand different feelings swirl around inside me.

Then I hear the sound of slamming doors and crashing feet downstairs, and my heart stops. There's a lot of shouting going on, heavy footsteps ... and from the corner of my eye I can see Alice keeping perfectly still, her face frozen as she listens. She's covered with a film of sweat and she doesn't look so pretty any more. She looks heartless and cunning and greedy.

She looks like everyone else.

"Listen," she says. "They're coming ... they're coming up here."

I can hear the rungs of the ladder creaking, then the sound of a voice calling out. "Hello? Miss May ... Hello? Are you up there? Hello? This is the police ... we're armed. We're coming in now. OK? We're coming in."

CHAPTER 10
I DON'T KNOW

I have no thoughts now. I'm just a body. My head is empty and I'm living on my nerves.

I can hear every little sound. I can hear the police officers entering the attic, their quiet steps and careful whispering, the soft clank of gun metal, the groan of the floorboards. I can see them – in my mind, I can *see* them. I can see them in their bulletproof vests, their helmets, their visors. I can see them searching the attic for any signs of life, their torchlights sweeping over the beams and the rafters and the dusty old boxes piled up in dark corners. And I can feel them, too. Nothing happens. Then, as they come to see that Alice isn't here, their voices get louder. They start to move around more freely, and the sense of danger begins to fade.

In front of me, Alice is staring hard at the wall. Her green eyes are wide open. Her hand is gripping the pistol. She's breathing hard. She's sweating hard. I can see the rise and fall of her chest. I can hear the gasp of her short, shallow breaths.

"Hey," says a voice from outside. "Look at that."

"What?"

"The wall ... there's a hole in the wall."

"Christ!" someone says.

Then they're all hurrying over to the wall. I imagine them all examining the hole, peering through into the attic next door. And one of them says, "She's gone through here ... she's gone into the house next door. Is it covered?"

"I don't know, sir."

"Well, find out – now!"

And then I hear the sound of radios, squawking voices, people moving quickly ... and I guess they're doing just what Dad said they'd do. They think that Alice has escaped through the house next door.

Dad was right.

Damn it.

He was right.

Now, as Dad's plan begins to work, and the police start chasing around in the wrong direction, making lots of noise, I feel Alice's hand on my leg. I look up to see her leaning towards me with a smile on her face. Her hands are empty. The gun is resting on top of the rucksack. Her skin is pale, hot, shining with sweat.

"I think this is going to work," she whispers. "I think it's going to *work*."

"Yeah?" I say.

And she nods, her face lit up with some kind of joy – and that's when I scream and jump at her.

It's not much of a fight, but then I don't want it to be. I'm not trying to beat her up or anything. I'm just trying to keep her away from the gun until the police can get in here.

So I've jumped on top of her and knocked the breath from her lungs, and I'm shouting and yelling as loud as I can – "HEY! HEY! IN HERE! IN THE CHIMNEY! BEHIND THE WARDROBE!" – and I've grabbed the gun off the rucksack and thrown it across the floor.

Now she starts to fight back. She's got her lungs working again, she's got over the shock, and she's fighting mad. Fighting like an animal – screaming, hissing, spitting, cursing ... punching me, scratching my face ... she's even trying to bite me. I'm trying to pin her down on the floor, but it's like trying to pin down a nest of snakes. She's only small, but she's strong and quick and agile, and I haven't got enough hands to control her.

"HURRY UP!" I'm shouting. "PLEASE ... HURRY! HELP ME!!"

I can hear them now, breaking into the wardrobe, crashing through all the stuff that Dad piled up in there.

'Won't be long now,' I think. 'It won't be long –'

"Bastard!" spits Alice, and she knees me in the groin, which hurts like hell.

I lose my grip on her arms, and she reaches up and rakes her fingernails down my face, drawing blood. My eyes are shut tight against the pain, and I'm groping blindly, trying to get hold of her arm, but my hand is caught up in something … the straps of her rucksack. My right hand is caught up in the straps of her rucksack. And now she's squirming out from under me, wriggling like a mad thing, reaching across for her gun. I try to hold her back with only one hand, but I need both hands. So, as hard as I can, I start yanking my right hand around, trying to untangle it, and somehow it ends up inside the rucksack.

I'm losing it now, losing control, and fear is taking over … and that gives me the extra spur that I need.

By using my legs and my body, I've somehow kept Alice held back, but I can see her fingers edging towards the gun, getting closer and closer all the time. The police are still struggling around in the wardrobe, and my hand is still stuck in the rucksack. I know I'm in trouble if I don't do something soon.

Fear gives me the power to twist my body and flip myself backwards and upwards. With a loud grunt of effort, I'm upside down in the air, looking up through the chimney at a circle of sky, and then down I come, back first, landing hard on Alice's head. I hear a dull crack, a groan, and then everything goes quiet.

The seconds pass ... ten seconds, maybe twenty ... I don't know.

I'm dazed and out of breath. Soaked in sweat, covered with soot. I'm lying on my back, on Alice's head. I'm pulling my hand from the rucksack. I'm doing something ...

My eyes are closed.

I don't know what I'm doing.

Then the back of the wardrobe bursts open, and I'm staring up at a blinding light and into the barrel of a policeman's gun.

CHAPTER 11
LIKE DAD SAID

And that's just about it. That's my story. That's
what happened to me on that hot summer
Saturday in June. It seems a long time ago now,
but it isn't – it's only been about two weeks. Ten
days, come to think of it. Or maybe it's eleven?

I don't know.

I seem to have lost track of time.

Anyway, you don't have to know all the details
of what happened after that. But I will tell you
what happened to Alice.

She wasn't badly hurt when I jumped on her
head. She was just knocked out for a bit. The
police put handcuffs on her and took her away. I
haven't seen her again. I think she's in for stealing

a motorbike, armed robbery and illegal possession of a gun ... and that's just for starters.

I guess she'll be locked away for a while.

The police are still investigating Dad and Grandad.

I told the cops everything about them – the money, the deal they had with Alice, the way they used me as insurance ... I even helped the cops look for the money. Alice was right – Dad and Grandad had hidden it away. I've spent a lot of time in Grandad's house, and I know about most of the hiding places. It didn't take long to find the money. It wasn't much, after all. I don't know how much, exactly, but I saw the cash when they found it, and it didn't look like a fortune to me. A few thousand pounds, perhaps – four or five grand, something like that. So, if they had a third, the total cash Alice took couldn't have been more than fifteen grand. Not that anyone seems to know the exact figure.

But more of that in a minute.

Like I said, the police are still looking into what Dad and Grandad have been up to. They're not in prison and I expect they're back in Grandad's house. I'm not sure what's going to happen to them. Not much, I expect. They'll wriggle their way out of things. They always do. But as long as they don't bother me, I don't care what happens to them.

Poor old Graq's been moved into an old people's home. Social Services took him away when Dad and Grandad were locked up. I visited him two days ago, but I don't think I'll go again. All he did was stare at the horse-racing on TV and mumble away about chips. I don't think he even knew who I was.

And me? What happened to me?

Well, I had to answer a lot of questions, and I had to make a statement. I'll have to go to court when Alice has her trial ... but apart from that, nothing much has changed. Well, *some* things have changed. I don't have to visit Dad any more. So all my Saturdays are free, which is very nice.

What else?

Oh yeah. I had a phone call from Amy. She rang me one night and asked if I still wanted to meet up with her some time.

"Why?" I asked her.

"Why?"

"Yeah – why?"

"Well," she said. "I just thought it'd be nice."

"You didn't think it'd be nice before."

"I know, but –"

"No, thanks," I said, and I put the phone down.

I don't know what she thought about that. I don't really care. You see, I've got a new girlfriend now. Her name's Tara. She's a year older than me, with long dark hair and stunning brown eyes and a figure that takes your breath away. I met her in a club. She wasn't too keen on me at first, but when she saw all the cash in my wallet, she suddenly changed her mind. Pretty shallow, I know.

But who cares?

I mean, she's *beautiful*.

I *like* being with her.

I *like* spending my money on her.

All right, I know it's not strictly my money, but I don't feel guilty about it. It's not as if I meant to take it from Alice's rucksack when I was lying on her head in the chimney. I was dazed and confused, remember? My hand had a life of its own. When I finally yanked it out of the rucksack, the bundle of cash was already there, gripped tight in my fingers. I couldn't do anything about it. Before I knew what was happening, my hand had stuffed the cash down the back of my trousers.

Then, the next thing I knew, the police were all over the place, pointing guns at me and shining lights in my eyes ... and, in all the fuss, I suppose I must have forgotten about it. When I did remember ... well, it was too late. Think of all the explaining I would have had to do ... and all the problems I would have had.

In the end, I decided the best thing to do was just keep the money.

It's hard to believe, I know.

But there you go.

No one seems to have noticed the missing cash. The Co-op aren't complaining, and the police haven't asked me about it. Which makes me think that they don't know how much was stolen in the first place. The only person who knows about it is Alice, and I don't think she's said anything. I don't know why not. She knows how much she stole. She counted it out on the table. She must know how much they're saying she stole. She must know that some of it's missing. So why hasn't she said anything?

Don't ask me.

I don't know.

And I don't think I *want* to know, either.

Like Dad said, as long as she keeps her mouth shut ...

Everything will be all right.

ABOUT KEVIN BROOKS

Kevin Brooks was born in Exeter and now lives in North Yorkshire with his wife Susan and a bunch of animals. Before he became a full-time author of hard-hitting, compelling teen fiction, Kevin did too many things to mention and lived in too many places to remember. He has been a rock star, worked in a zoo, a crematorium and a post office. Kevin's brilliant novels have won many awards, most notably the 2014 Carnegie Medal for *The Bunker Diary*.

'Kevin Brooks just gets better and better' *Sunday Telegraph*

'A masterly writer' *Mail on Sunday*

Praise for *Johnny Delgado: Private Detective*

'The breathtaking pace of the end of the book brings it to an energetic conclusion, but it is the subtext of compassion, loyalty and justice which ultimately gives the book its resonance' *Books for Keeps*

Praise for *The Bunker Diary*

'An exceptional, brave book that pulls no punches and offers no comfortable ending' *CILIP Carnegie Medal Judges*

Our books are tested
for children and young people by
children and young people.

Thanks to everyone who consulted on
a manuscript for their time and effort in
helping us to make our books better
for our readers.